"..." : The Unknown Darkness

Vol. I

Poetry

"..."

Dedicated to my grandma
Who has always loved these

To my sisters...
We'll get through this together

And dedicated to Charlie
Who deserved better

I love you guys

Angelina Valencia

Never be ashamed
about being
broken, because
strength is nothing
but pain that's
been repaired

- Trent Shelton

"..."

Table of Contents

Silence

Silence isn't an option
It's about finding the right words
And even when it's found
It's a matter of being heard

I wish I could say that I know
How I'm feeling inside
But I simply don't know
I swear I've tried

I don't like being vulnerable
I like being strong
But what if all this time
I was wrong?

I wish I could put this heart
Up for adoption
I'm trying but I swear
Silence isn't my option

Wounds

When a wound first shows
You have to let it heal
Even when it hurts
Sometimes it's best to conceal
Stop opening your wounds
Your pain cannot reveal
I know you want to love
And I know you want to feel
Stop choosing things that break you
And start choosing what is real
You keep choosing things that cut you
Then your wound will never seal
Even if they take your heart
It's your soul they cannot steal
So stop touching your wounds
Or they will never heal

A Package

I have a package for you
Might take you by surprise
But it's in a box
It's bigger than its normal size

It's coming your way
But when you get it
Don't leave it
Or forget it

It's all I have left to give
Most people break it
But I trust you enough
I'm asking you to take it

Take good care of it for me
It's a piece of me, the best part
The box will read "Fragile"
And inside you'll find my heart

"..."

Heartache

Weight on your shoulders
A hole in your chest
Anxiety hits you
And turns you into a mess

A burn in your body
Uncontrollable tears
Sleepless nights
Added more fears

You have no mood
Just a overthinking head
You don't feel hungry
So you don't eat instead

You feel hurt inside
But it's not a heartbreak
This is what it feels like
To have a heartache

<u>sHE beLIEveD</u>

He lied…
But yet once again
He'll say he loved her
He'll take her out on dates
It's not his first time
He'll keep playing games
While on the other hand
She'll continue falling hard
She thinks about him every minute
She'll listen to songs that remind her of him
And wished he was there
She continued to love
She believed…

Now read bottom to top

Trust me

Trust me when I say
I'm fine
I'm just drowning in music
And understanding every line

Trust me when I tell you
I'm okay
I swear I only feel
Hurt and lonely today

Trust me when I say
I'm good
I only need earbuds
And a jacket with a hood

Trust me when I tell you
I'm great
It's only been the third day
I ate nothing on my plate

Trust me when I say
Never been better
I've only been filling envelopes
With countless letters

So trust me when I tell you
That I have been trying
Because only every time you ask
I've been lying

<u>She...</u>

I see this girl everyday...

She puts on that smile
But she's hiding in every way...

She pushes out that laugh
But she wants that pain to go away...

She tells everyone leave her alone
But inside she's wishing they would stay...

She doesn't wear her heart on her sleeve
Cause' she don't want to show that it's broken
on display...

She may say she's fine
But it don't mean everything's okay...

It may be all sunny outside
But she feels that everything is gray...

People notice the change
They tell her that they pray and pray

But she hides all her thoughts

And doesn't listen to what they say…

People, it's the pain…
It kills her everyday…

"…"

<u>I'm not okay</u>

This pain inside
Is something that's not okay
I don't know where it comes from
Or why I feel this way

Its hit me deep inside
Causing me to lie
I tell them I'm fine
Nothing works when I try

There's something missing
Something I need
This hurt that's growing
Is sprouting from its seed

Help me before I give up
Help me before I fall
I may seem okay
But I'm not at all…

Angelina Valencia

This side of my skin

This side of my skin
Is what you see
But what is underneath
Is the real me

You'll see me smile
But I cry inside
You'll see me laugh
But my butterflies have died

I may say I'm fine
But not when I'm alone
Shadows beat me down
But the bruises are never shown

This side of my skin
Is what you see
But what's underneath…
It kills me

Flower

Sometimes I want to be a flower
I'd get to be in the sun
Or in the rain
So I wouldn't have to run

I'd also get picked
So I won't be alone
I'd be given or used
And then I'd be tossed or thrown

But just for that one second
I was loved and wanted
It's better than calling for help
When no one has responded

<u>Storms</u>

I know you're not okay
You can say you are
But remember what I told you?
When I said you're the star?

Don't let anxiety get to you
Don't let burdens run your head
Your emotions run high
You think things that were never said

Just take a deep breath
And remember who you are
You had past trauma
And it's always going to be a scar

But someone once said
Not every storm came to attack
Some storms came
To clear your path

Underwater

Under the waters is where I feel best
All the sounds get out of my ears
As the water flows into my chest
I let it mix with my tears

I begin to hear the pounding in my head
Warning me I need air
I could just sit there and drown instead
It's not like I'm going anywhere

You say you'd save me
But how can you when you're not here
You instead chose to leave
You just disappeared

So yes, I'm drowning now
Slowly into the unknown black night
Maybe I'll come back somehow
Or I'll just turn white

Behind the trigger

Your words were your advice
Your smile kept me going
But you became a different person
Without me even knowing

Your heart was no longer in place
Gunpowder was only there
So every word that you spoke
Sent a bullet in the air

Every hug that you gave
Left a poison stain
Causing every ounce of love
Only to be pain

I never even noticed
Since my trust was getting bigger
So I never saw it coming
When you were behind the trigger

Fake Crown

My loyalty pointed to you
I bent on one knee
I gave you all I had
But you didn't want me

I don't want your crown
Made of silver and gold
I don't want your love
It was always cold

You lead your armies
To try and win me back
But see I lead my armies
To prepare for an attack

You can't fool me
With the games you play
You keep thinking you'll win
But surely not today

So again, my loyalty pointed to you
I bowed my head down
Don't ask for me back
You can keep your fake crown

<u>Six feet under</u>

Somethings wrong with me
My insides are dying
No I don't mean physically...
Okay maybe I'm lying

It just feels like something is
Pulling out my heart
But first it feels like
Piece by piece it's pulling it apart

Then puts weight on my shoulders
To where my legs give out
Then while I lay on the floor
I get burned while I scream and shout

I don't really care just
Put me six feet under the ground
Put me out of my misery
So no one will hear my screaming sound

"..."

If I couldn't speak

If I couldn't speak
Would you be able to hear me?

Would you understand
The words of my song?
When I don't speak
Can you sing along?

Would you understand me
When I say I love you?
Would you say it back?
Say I love you too?

When I call for help
Through our eyes
Would you come and save me?
Or watch me slowly die?

Tell me, what you would do
If I couldn't speak?

Angelina Valencia

Depression

Depression hits you badly
You might think you want to be dead
But it's that type of feeling
That puts your hoodie over your head

You feel down
Almost feel no mood
You find nothing to be funny
And no appetite of food

You want to disappear from the world
You feel left out
So you want to sleep forever
Or scream and shout

Instead you put your headphones in your ears
Drown all that annoys you
Then close your eyes
And wait till depression destroys you

Playing with emotions

You play with my emotions
Like I don't have any
Keep me crying tears
Trust me, I have plenty

You were my everything
But it's like you don't care
You want to be here for me
But you're never there

You want to take me out
We even stay up all night
But it seems like you like to hurt
Everything that felt right

You make it hard to fall in love
With someone else when you're still here
Me still loving you
Makes my pain more severe

I know somewhere inside
I hope you still feel the same
I even prove it
By putting up with your games

<u>The end of someone's daughter</u>

It's not fun being hurt
Sometimes people don't even know
It feels like I'm drowning underwater
Like my head is going to explode

Is it really that hard?
To tell when I'm hurt?
I mean yeah I'll admit
This isn't my first

But I've walked through so many crowds
No one even bothered to look
The shadows towered over me
Ready to end my book

This is it
The end of someone's daughter
Because slowly
I am drowning in the water

Mask

Behind the mask is where you hide
You don't show yourself
You keep your hands tied

You don't realize there is someone out there
Trust is hard to come
But just continue to breathe the air
And try not to be so numb

You don't want to cry in front of others
So you push them away
You might find it hard to talk to sisters and
brothers
So you go the other way

Or maybe when you wake up
Your chest starts to hurt
No one will fill up your cup
So you're more alert

It starts to get worse and worse
You hate how it feels
Keep telling yourself you're cursed
And that maybe time heals

Then you begin to ask
'What if it never goes away?'
But it's that mask...
It kills you everyday

I don't know

I don't know
What the future holds
I don't know
If I'll die young or old
I don't know
Why I feel this way
I don't know
Why I'm not okay
I don't know
Why people decide to change
I don't know
Why I feel so strange
I don't know
If you'll ever feel the same
I don't know
Why I feel this pain
Oh wait I do
It's all because of you

Angelina Valencia

It really hurts

It really hurts
When I first met you
I had the time of my life
When it was just us two

Until someone broke you
Those pieces were tossed
And that someone took one
While the others were lost

So you'll never be whole again
But you can't stand here this very day
Look me in the eyes
And tell me that everything is okay

It's okay to tell the truth
Even when it hurts
All you have to know
Is that I was with you first

So throw that person away
The pain is closing around your throat
Put back that smile on your face
Because that person has hurt you the most

"..."

Does not belong

There's always something missing
And yet I can never find
I tried fitting every puzzle
And none of them were ever mine

I tried searching beyond the known
Behind shadows and closed doors
I looked far inside wells
And even dug deep underneath floors

I looked everywhere for the missing piece
Inside eyes that were shy
I looked everywhere on this earth
But yet nothing could make me fly

So I thought something would fit this piece
But it turns out I was wrong
See there is no fitting puzzle
For my heart does not belong

<u>Love yourself first</u>

You smile
But yet you cry
You say you're fine
But yet you want to die

You say it's funny
But yet you don't laugh
You say you have a big heart
But yet it's split in half

You talk
But yet you want to be silent
You act like you've never been better
But at home it's violent

You stay in crowded areas
But yet you want to be alone
You've got to stop giving out love
That you don't keep as your own

Real pain

Pain isn't just tears
Or the feeling of being down
Pain isn't wearing a fake smile
Or wearing a real frown

Pain isn't the feeling of a papercut
Or even a knife
Sure it will hurt like hell
But isn't that life?

Pain isn't an ache in your body
Or not eating for days
Pain isn't an emotion
That can just be put away

Pain is looking in the mirror
Saying it's going to get better
Tears streaming down your face
Begging yourself to hold it together

Angelina Valencia

Dear person who broke me

I admit, inside I'm still hurt
And that's never going to go away
Ask me how I'm doing
I promise I'm okay
These tears aren't worth nothing
There's a reason why I cry everyday
Maybe I was just an experiment
I guess I didn't pass the survey
It's funny because
You drop on your knees and pray
But then come home to just
Drop pain on my plate
There are so many things I think
But no words left to say
I have no more coins
For these games that you play
You ripped me in pieces
But yet I don't hate
Isn't it weird how it works?
How I expected you to stay?
I have the biggest heart
But you chose mine to break?
I just really hope
Someone doesn't break me this way
Been through this once

"..."

Please don't turn my world grey

Our demons

Through the mist in the dark
Every shadow that is drawn
The demons are too quiet
But yet they're never gone

But when it's dark in my room
They laugh louder than before
And I'm constantly screaming
I don't want this anymore

But no one ever answers
No one's ever there
They keep the good doors locked
Just to leave me in despair

So when I am alone
The demons hug me and say
"No one loves you like us
We're the only ones who'll stay"

Paths broken

So the girl he did not meet
Left his heartbroken and incomplete
Though their paths will never meet
And because his happiness is what he did not
see
His heart continued to plea
For all the loss that he had conceived
But he knows he can never grieve
For he could never perceive
The happiness and a world of release

He thought it to be set in stone
But things in life are never left alone
For death and loss are similar
But the real pain is never shown
He never had someone to call his own
Since he was always hit with sticks and stones
Now his pain has always grown
While his burdens wear the throne
Perhaps his name was never known
Since he will always be alone

Also written by David Buchanan

<u>Somewhere I can breathe</u>

Sometimes I want to disappear
Not get buried beneath
But somewhere alone
Where I can breathe

I want to go somewhere
Not above or below
But somewhere far
Where no one will ever know

I want complete silence
Not with the dead
But someplace where
I can't hear my own head

I just want to disappear
Not somewhere I cannot be seen
But just somewhere alone
Where I can breathe

Something I didn't mean

Nothing is worse
Then saying something you don't mean
But then they tell you
What you would've never seen
They say they don't need you
It's like there was no in-between
I faced my worse fear
And yet my hands are never clean
I want to go back
Give me the time machine
I don't want to know this person anymore
I thought she was my queen
Turns out she don't want to fight
For me
She gave up and said
It's me she don't need
Said have a good life
But she was my routine
Only thing I woke up to
What turned my mood green
I lost myself and I said something that wasn't
true
But I guess some things are meant to be
I thought it would be her
Thought that was the shoulder I would lean

Angelina Valencia

Turns out the pain stays
When you're still a teen

<u>Every now and then</u>

Every now and then
I cry to myself
And every now and then
I cry out for help

Every now and then
I swallow down my pain
But I didn't know
It put poison in my veins

So every now and then
I wonder where you are
I wonder what you're doing
When I know you aren't far

Every now and then
My heart begins to hurt
My head begins to pound
When you should've put me first

But yet every now and then
You try and win me back
But in the back of my mind
Your love was pitch black

<u>Silently</u>

Silently...
...The tears stream down

Silently...
...Screams for help

Silently...
...Walks down the hall

Silently...
...Pushes herself away

Silently...
...Drifts away

Silently...
...She falls apart...

Mixed signals

You act like you care
Then you act like you don't
You say you'll take care of me
Then you say you won't

You'd text me 'Morning'
And I'll text you right back
But then I don't get a reply
Until the day turns black

You say you want to take me out
So I say that we can
But then somethings come up
So you want to change the plan

Stop giving mixed signals
Just say you want to be friends
Trust me it's easier
Then trying to pretend

I am who I am

If I want your help
Then I gave up trying
If I want the truth
Then I'm tired of you lying

If I want to see you
Then I'm probably alone
Or maybe I miss you
Since you don't hit up my phone

If I tell you I'm sorry
Then I messed up bad
If I tell you I'm staying
Then you're all I have

If I miss your hugs
It's because yours were the best
If I tell you I love you
I'm only trying to express

So if I tell you my past
Don't feel sorry or say 'damn'
I'm telling you so
You know why I am who I am

Eating disorder

Another hour without eating
Another time without drinking
Endless days with only sleeping
And countless nights with only thinking

She looks in the mirror with insecurity
She's down to skin and bone
But beyond the eyes of what is there
She sees bigger than what is shown

There'll be times where little she'll eat
Making her body believe
But over the toilet she'll stand
Forcing the food the leave

To be the skinniest girl alive
She thinks it's greater than it sounds
So she slowly gets weaker and weaker
Till she's down to 80 pounds

Some don't make it through
Others are forced to fight
So fix yourself up now
And choose to do what's right

Angelina Valencia

Not made to be understood

What if I'm made to understand?
Be there when people need me
Made to say the right words
But yet no one can read me

I can give the best hugs
And give you all that I own
Be your advice when you need it
But yet I am left alone

I can pick up your broken pieces
And put them where they belong
I can plant a smile on your face
But yet I can't be that strong

I can be your shoulder
And be there more than I should
But what I don't get is
Why I am not made to be understood

My life is like music

My life is like music
It gets stuck in my head
I try and think of another
But it gets replayed instead

The music is put on records
Then on the shelf they're put away
But even though I have it on shuffle
It gets played every day

Why am I constantly reminded
Of the same stuff every time?
I want to hear something new
Something that doesn't rhyme

I'm tired of the same life
Where everything I do is wrong
Stop playing the same lines
And give me a new song

Knife

It feels like my heart is dead
It feels like I'm dying
Why does it hurt my head?
Why am I lying?

You ask me how I'm doing
You ask me how I feel
Well, deep down I'm losing
To what I thought was real

I can't sleep at night
I just feel the worst
Nothing feels right
My chest just hurts

Just forget about me
Go live your life
Live your love free
I'll just... play with this knife...

Would you do the same?

I'd travel through time
I'd travel through space
Just to be there for you
In the time that it takes

I may not be the best
But I know I'm not the worse
Just let me hold your hand
At the times when it hurts

I'd take the fall
And I'd take my life
I'd do anything
To make things right

So I'd take a bullet
And I'd take the blame
My only question is
Would you do the same?

Changed

Don't tell me I'm different
Don't tell me I've changed
You broke my heart
Well, what was remained

Don't tell me what to do
Don't tell me what I need
I fed you love to heal
The wounds that you bleed

But clearly you wasted
All that I gave
You broke through my wall
And entered my waves

It's funny because
I've been through this before
But it's like all the pain
Doesn't hurt anymore

The one good thing

It sucks when you're lonely
It's like the walls close in on you
You keep wondering if only…
Nah…your love wasn't true

But then why do I spend my time
Letting the thoughts eat me up?
This ladder I had to climb
Was just to fill up your cup

That's not what I want
I want someone real
Not someone who spends their time to haunt
The one good thing is what you steal

But honestly it's all good
I'll find someone new
Someone in the future
That's better than you

Angelina Valencia

An 'end' in 'friend'

There's an 'end' in 'friend'
We've all heard that
But deciding who stays in our lives
Is our combat

There's a 'good' in 'goodbye'
That's something we all knew
But why it is good
Is all up to you

There's a 'lie' in 'believe'
But that's all that they do
They scan through the crowd
And they pick and choose

There's 'hell' in 'hello'
It could be your worst mistake
It's not always bad
But it could be your first heartbreak

There are all these things
Most hit like a knife
But the scariest of them all
Is there's an 'if' in 'life'

Hate me alone

Fake stories and starting rumors
Is not how it should be
Don't go telling stuff
When you don't know the whole story

It's cool that you don't like me
But don't make a scene
Just keep it to yourself
You make a problem bigger then it seems

Just leave me in my corner
Without fingers pointing to me
Stop whispering in each other's ears
I'm begging you so, please

If you hate me
Just hate me alone
You've got everyone to turn against me
Just so you can wear the throne

<u>Deep inside</u>

Somewhere deep inside
Is something I cannot explain
It gets me every night
It's what I call pain

It sometimes breaks me down
Other times it affects my society
And yet here I am
Filled with anxiety

I may say I'm fine
I may smile and laugh
Its cause the demon
Is my other half

Go ahead and leave me
They do everyday
I'm used to it
Nobody loves me anyway

Fought for

I stood in the arena
Prepared for any fight
I've lost some battles
But I've won what's right

I've fought until I was
Down to skin and bone
Yet somehow the crowd never cheered
I was always left alone

I have a mind of my own
Trust me it's loud
Yet I've got nothing left standing
It's just a dark cloud

I always ask myself
Why can't it be like before?
Its time I stop fighting for you
I want to be fought for

She was beautiful

She was beautiful
And no, not for her looks
She was beautiful
And not from fantasy books

She was beautiful
It was all on the inside
She was beautiful
Even with the things that died

She was beautiful
With the way she spoke her words
She was beautiful
Her love was like a song from every bird

She was beautiful
With all the things she thought
She was beautiful
After every battle she fought

She was beautiful
Until it was herself she couldn't find
Why did that person
Leave her behind

"..."

The day love died

The day I stopped crying
Still hasn't come
You'd think after these years
I'd forget what I've done

But yet I still hear voices in my head
Telling me I'm no good
Even the broken ones tend to smile
Even more than I could

So the day you came back
Was the day you walked away
You made me lie to everyone
And say I'm okay

Now my world no longer exist
All the growing seeds have dried
The day I stopped smiling
Was the day that love died

You never wanted to stay

I watched your footsteps
Disappear in the sand
You walked away with no hesitation
To hurt me seemed like your plan

I watched you smile
Every time you lied
You can't see inside
But the butterflies died

I watched your eyes
Turned into something new
My hesitant to love
Turned into eager too

But my eyes flooded
As I watched you walk away
I really fought for you
But you never wanted to stay

Head and Heart

"Come on I'm telling you
That's the one"

"But we don't even know
What they have done"

"I know that's the one
I can feel it inside"

"But we don't know
What they plan to hide"

"But they've got to be
It just feels so right"

"But what if they're something
Different at night"

"They could also be the
Person of your dreams"

"What if they're
Not all that they seem"

"I'm sure they're the one

They won't tear you apart"

And that was the conversation
Between a head and a heart

It's not

It's not a painting without paint
It's not kindness without giving
It's not a flower without sunlight
And it's not life without living

It's not love without pain
And it's not pain without suffer
You hear life will get better
But life will get tougher

It's not beauty without art
It's not death without grief
It's not money without greed
It's not crime without a thief

It's not feelings without emotion
It's not inspiring without speeches
It's not laughter without smiles
And it's not broken without pieces

Someone else instead

You can hear my heart beating
It's breaking through my ribs
Trying to be set free
From all that you did

My eyes begin to water
Even when I said I'm fine
But you still choose to walk away
So I no longer made you mine

It's still weird how I think of you
It's like I hate you but I love you at the same
time
I don't want you in my head
But it's like your memories want to climb and
climb

Maybe I should want you back?
But you don't understand me enough
I call for help through my head
But having it reach you is tough

I think it's time I stop thinking of you
So get out of my head
It's time for me to move on

"…"

And go think of someone else instead

Angelina Valencia

<u>Do you?</u>

Do you ever feel broken?
And hurt inside?
But you can't figure out
The reason why?

You listen to music
That puts you in the mood
You start to feel sad
And angry too

Do you feel that something is missing?
Like a piece of your life?
You begin to feel inside
Something like a sharp knife

Then just as someone fills in that puzzle
They go and turn away
How is it that
I'm still alive today

My dark side

The dark can be silent
But it can also be loud
I tend to feel alone
Even when I'm in a crowd

The dark is filled with secrets
That no one has yet to know
They're locked behind doors
And buried deep below

The dark reflects all
That I don't want to see
It reveals what defines
The dark side of me

My dark side
Might be filled with scars
But my dark side
Is also filled with stars

Reflection

Reflection, stop telling me I'm not good enough
Stop telling me I don't deserve to live
Stop telling me there's nothing to fight for
Stop telling me I've got nothing to give

Stop telling me I'm worth nothing
Stop telling me I'm wasting my life
Step telling me to stop breathing
Stop telling me to grab that knife

Stop pointing out all my flaws
Stop telling me my imperfections
Stop telling me my life in this world
Has no point or connection

Stop pointing out what I already know
You're making it harder for me to breath
I stare at you everyday
Just keep my flaws between you and me

Wrong

I feel alone
Consumed by the darkness that's
never-ending
I feel like I'm wasting
The time being nice that I'm spending

I try my best to make people happy
But they always choose to go away
Maybe being nice is wrong
Since no one ever chooses to stay

These past weeks I've had the same dream
Trapped in a dark room where it's cold
There's no sign of light in this place
I'm only left all alone

I question if people don't like me
If everything I do is wrong
What if all this time
Nobody liked me all along?
What if I lose you?

I worry you might leave me
I'm often known for my overthinking head
But what if someone else catches your eye

And you go fall for them instead?

What if one of these days
You decide I don't make you feel the same
way?
When the only thing I think about
Is you every day

What if all I give is too little
Or maybe too much?
Would I lose the sound of your voice?
The feeling of your touch?

Just what if I lose you?
It's a question that never goes away
You are my world
I'm just hoping you'll stay

You're telling me...?

Look me in the eyes and tell me
That I look okay
You can't see the emptiness in my eyes?
The dark clouds of grey?

You're telling me that you can't see
The strings attached to my lips?
It forces me to smile
By pulling it up from the tips

You're telling me that you can't see
My heart trying to break free?
Because it's trying to make more room
For the pain I hold inside me

Of course you can't see any of this
I don't know why I bothered to ask
Sometimes I forget that
I hide all these behind my mask

<u>You can't tell me how I'm feeling</u>

Every breath I inhale
Is a shudder through my spine
I know I always say the same
I know it's always an "I'm fine"

Sure maybe you don't believe me
Or maybe you don't care
You tell me you're here for me
But yet you're never there

Is it really worth telling you
My emotions throughout the days?
When I already know you're going to tell me
"It's just a phase"

I'm sorry but you don't know what it's like
You can't tell me how I'm feeling
If you attack me with every word you say
Then how am I going to begin healing?

Go after the best

Did I do something wrong?
To cause you to let go of my hand
To go with someone else's embrace
That's where I used to stand

Why did you give up on what was so real?
Why wasn't I enough for you to stay?
I told you I'm here for you and I still am
But for some reason you decided to push me
away

It's okay I'm happy for you
You enjoy their presence and embrace
It's just that it wasn't that long ago
When I was in that place

I'm still stuck in this corner though
I finally figured out why you left
It's because they're better looking
And so you go after the best

I'm afraid of living

I'm afraid of dying
I don't know what is waiting for me
I don't know if I'll be alone
If it's nothing but darkness I'll see

Will I still feel the pain I feel today?
Will it be worse than before?
The constant anxiety…
Will I have that anymore?

What if all I can do is scream?
Or what if I'm no longer there?
Erased from existence
What if no one cares?

Just what if all these scars
Are just the beginning
Maybe I'm not afraid of dying
Maybe I'm afraid of living

"…"

Coming Soon!

The Unknown Darkness Vol. II
Hidden Emotions
Angelina Valencia